COURAGE
ON ICE

BY JAKE MADDOX

text by
Veeda Bybee

STONE ARCH BOOKS
a capstone imprint

Jake Maddox JV Girls books are published by
Stone Arch Books
a Capstone imprint
1710 Roe Crest Drive
North Mankato, Minnesota 56003

www.capstonepub.com

Library of Congress Cataloging-in-Publication Data
Names: Maddox, Jake, author. | Bybee, Veeda, author. | Maddox, Jake. Jake
    Maddox JV girls.
Title: Courage on ice / by Jake Maddox ; text by Veeda Bybee.
Description: North Mankato, Minnesota : Stone Arch Books, [2019] | Series: Jake Maddox.
    Jake Maddox JV girls | Summary: Late for practice at the ice arena, thirteen-year-old Eva
    Chen neglects to warm up and suffers a concussion when she falls during a difficult jump.
    Frustrated at missing practice time and worried about doing her routine at the family
    showcase, in front of a full arena, her parents, and her grandmother, Eva does not need
    any extra threats to her confidence—for instance, discovering that some of the other girls
    are laughing at her Chinese heritage.
Identifiers: LCCN 2019008758| ISBN 9781496584700 (hardcover) | ISBN 9781496584724 (pbk.)
    | ISBN 9781496584748 (ebook pdf)
Subjects: LCSH: Chinese American figure skaters—Juvenile fiction. | Chinese American
    families—Juvenile fiction. | Figure skating stories. | Brain—Concussion—Juvenile fiction.
    | Self-confidence—Juvenile fiction. | Bullying—Juvenile fiction. | Grandmothers—
    Juvenile fiction. | CYAC: Chinese Americans—Fiction. | Ice skating—Fiction. | Brain—
    Concussion—Fiction. | Self-confidence—Fiction. | Bullying—Fiction. | Grandmothers—
    Fiction.
Classification: LCC PZ7.M25643 Cn 2019 | DDC 813.6 [Fic] —dc23
LC record available at https://lccn.loc.gov/2019008758

Designer: Dina Her

Image Credits:
Shutterstock: cluckva, (geometric) design element throughout, Eky Studio, (stripes) design
element throughout, sportpoint, Cover, Vit Kovalcik, (skates) design element throughout

Printed in the United States of America.
PA70

TABLE OF CONTENTS

CHAPTER 1

THE PERFECT SONG

Eva Chen spread her arms wide, as if she were greeting everyone at the Snow Castles Ice Arena. Even though she shared the ice with other skaters this cold morning, she liked to pretend that she was the only one on the ice.

Stroke, stroke, stroke.

Eva pushed her feet forward. She felt her muscles waking up. With her hands outstretched for balance, she glanced over her shoulder. She couldn't see it, but she knew her skates left tiny lines in the smooth, white ice.

White, like the color of the Chinese bao buns her grandmother made for her school lunch.

Grumble, grumble, grumble.

Eva placed a gloved hand on her stomach and felt the fluffy material of her fleece sweatshirt. Thinking about food made the thirteen-year-old remember that she had forgotten to eat breakfast. She shivered. She was hungry *and* cold. Eva rubbed her hands together. Even with her gloves, they felt as chilly as the hard ice beneath her.

Eva knew that after a few minutes of skating, her body temperature would rise. Usually when she stepped onto the ice, she was much warmer. She was supposed to do warm-ups before she started skating. They helped get her ready to exercise. Today, though, she decided to skip warming up to make up for lost time.

Eva had slept in past her alarm. Five a.m. was so early to wake up! And she was in such a rush that she also almost forgot her skates.

Eva yawned. She took early morning private lessons a couple of times a week with Coach Jo. On Saturdays she had group lessons. Eva had been skating since she was five years old. She didn't think missing one warm-up would be a big deal. They were boring anyway. All she did in warm-ups was stretch and sometimes take a jog around the rink. Eva would rather be on the ice, doing turns, crossovers, and skating. These moves made figure skating fun, not warm-ups.

She went around the rink again—this time in the opposite direction. The more her legs moved, the faster she picked up speed. Even with the cold air of the rink nipping at her face, she could feel her cheeks warming. Eva loved the feeling of going fast on the ice. It almost felt like flying.

There were several other girls on the ice practicing on their own or with coaches. Her best friend, Jazz Mason, was already tucking in for a camel spin.

Jazz was great at spinning. One leg was straight behind her, parallel to the ice. Her body was stretched out like the shape of the letter T. Jazz looked forward as she spun.

"Way to go, Jazz!" Eva said, gliding next to her. She watched Jazz give one last twirl.

Classical music floated through the sound system as Stephanie Watson skated her routine. The song was slow and elegant. When the orchestra picked up speed, Stephanie's ponytail whipped behind her as she started a backward crossover.

"Stephanie is so good," Eva said to Jazz. She could hear the jealousy in her own voice. She thought of the other girls on the ice. She wanted to be powerful like Jazz. Or graceful like Stephanie.

Eva thought about her figure-skating routine for the upcoming family showcase. The event was a fun performance when all the ice skaters showed their families what they would be performing during the season.

Eva planned on doing an axel jump in her number. Maybe it would be just as beautiful as the other girls' skating.

Jazz skated alongside Eva. "Did Stephanie have to pick this song?" Jazz said. "It's pretty, but I feel like everyone skates to it."

Jazz had a point. Eva had heard this classical piece at many performances.

"What are you skating to?" Eva asked Jazz.

Jazz grinned. "A jazz number, of course!"

Both girls laughed. Of course Jazz would pick an upbeat song. In addition to matching her name, it fit her personality. Jazz was a strong skater, full of power and spunk.

"What about you, Eva?" Jazz said.

Eva crossed her skates in front of each other. "I'm doing a song I heard in a movie. It's 'Yellow,' by Coldplay, but the lyrics are sung by Katherine Ho in Mandarin."

"Cool!" Jazz said.

"Yeah, it's one of my parents' favorite songs, so when they heard it in Chinese, they really liked it. I thought it would be perfect for the family showcase, since my grandmother is coming. She'll actually understand the Chinese words."

"How is your grandma doing?" asked Jazz.

A few weeks ago, Eva's grandmother, or Ama, as she called her, had come to live with the Chen family. She had always lived far away in San Francisco. When Eva's grandfather passed away last year, Eva's mom knew that Ama wouldn't be able to stay on her own much longer.

Even though both of Eva's parents were Chinese, she didn't grow up speaking the language. Eva knew only a few words in Mandarin. Ama knew only a few words in English. So when Eva talked to Ama, one of her parents usually had to translate. Sometimes it was just easier to not say anything at all.

"She's okay," Eva said to Jazz. "My mom says she misses walking around Chinatown and being on her own. Here everything is in English and she feels lost all the time. She sits at home a lot and does a lot of origami."

"I love origami," Jazz said. "I can only make fortune tellers."

"Ama can make really cool stuff," Eva said. "Like animals or flowers. She's tried to teach me, but it's really hard. Especially since I have no idea what she's saying."

When Eva was picking a song for the family performance, she decided this special Mandarin arrangement might be a way for her to communicate with Ama. She knew it could be very special. Her performance number had words her grandmother could understand, with music her parents and most people were familiar with. It was the perfect way to share her love of skating with her whole family.

Eva waved goodbye to Jazz and decided to do some spins of her own. She leaned over to wind up for a scratch spin. Holding her arms and one leg out high, she spun, making circles in the ice. Pulling her limbs in closer, Eva spun faster and faster. Eva felt the thrill of her speed. She was glad she skipped her warm-up this morning. Getting right into skating was so much better.

To close and stop the spin, she finished in the landing position, with one leg out and her arms extended.

"Good job!" Coach Jo said from the rink side. "Those were some tight circles on the ice."

Eva took a big breath. "I love the scratch spin. I can go on forever."

"I noticed you haven't practiced any jumping yet," Coach Jo said. "Your axel will be a great moment in your family showcase. It will set the tone of the season and show everyone what you can do."

"The axel still makes me a little nervous," Eva said.

"It's a difficult jump," Coach Jo said. "But you've done it before, don't forget that. We already know you are physically capable of making the jump."

"Yeah, I know," Eva said.

"One other thing," Coach added. "Sometimes dedicating a performance or move to someone can help with your motivation. Is there someone you would like to skate for?"

Eva tugged on the fingers of her glove. "My grandma hasn't seen me skate. She might like seeing what I can do."

Coach Jo smiled. "Of course she will. You're skating from a place that is very personal. It will show on the ice."

Coach Jo stepped on the rink and waved to Eva. "Now come on. Let's get started."

Eva skated away from the edge and back to the center. It was time to practice her jump. She wanted to get it right for her coach, her season, and her grandma.

CHAPTER 2

LATE

The next morning Eva was late to practice. Again.

She managed to grab a muffin as she headed out the door. By the time she got to the rink, she knew she was even later than she had been for her last practice. In the car, Eva said a quick goodbye to her mother and raced inside.

She pulled on her skates and walked as fast as she could over to where the other figure skaters were already practicing. Most of them were all warmed up and had moved on to practicing their performance numbers.

One of the rink employees handed her a blue sash. "Last one," he said. "You're late."

The sashes were numbered to show the order in which the girls would practice their solo dance numbers for the showcase. The other skaters made room in the center of the ice for each girl to practice.

Eva tugged the sash over her sweatshirt and got ready to step onto the ice. There was no way she had time to warm up today.

As Eva took her first glides, Jazz skated up to her.

"Good morning!" Jazz said. She pointed to the sash across Eva's chest. "What number are you?"

Eva looked down. "Nine, the very last one."

Jazz was number two. She had already done her performance.

Stephanie's classical song started. Eva saw her take her starting position in the center of the rink. Stephanie was number seven. Eva's turn would be coming up soon. She knew she needed to start practicing, but she couldn't help but watch Stephanie.

The song picked up in tempo. Stephanie skated faster. She dug the tip of a blade in the ice and bent her knee, preparing for a flip jump. Turning her body around, Stephanie threw herself into the air. Pulling her arms in tight, she did a single rotation. When she landed, Stephanie spread her arms, holding them out to an imaginary crowd.

Eva watched Stephanie in awe. She knew she should be focusing on her own routine and not comparing herself with other skaters. But she couldn't help it. Stephanie was so graceful, and she made the flip jump look so easy. She moved along perfectly to the dramatic tempo of the music.

Eva hadn't seen Jazz practice, but she was sure her best friend had also skated well. She thought about her own jumps. Eva didn't think she was as skilled as Stephanie. Or as powerful as Jazz. The axel jump was her hardest move, and she wasn't entirely comfortable with it. Maybe putting it in her program was a bad idea.

Eva knew she should concentrate on her own routine. She needed to work on the axel jump, or else she might really mess up in front of everyone. Stephanie's song was coming to a close. Now only one skater was ahead of Eva.

Eva rubbed her hands together. She still felt cold. Without her warm-up, her body still felt a little stiff. But Eva didn't have time for stretching this morning.

She needed to get into her hard moves. Skipping a few boring minutes of warm-ups didn't hurt her last time. She was sure she would be fine today too.

Eva decided to go for it. Maybe if she just did the axel, she could stop worrying. She had landed it before; she could do it again right now.

Eva started by gliding backward. Each stroke was smooth and steady. As she turned into the jump, she felt herself holding her breath.

Her legs launched her up, and she aimed high. She held her hands together in front of her chest. Eva spun her body, making one and a half revolutions. But coming down for the landing, she knew her balance was off. She wasn't leaning on her right side, where her leg would touch the ice.

Her right skate slammed into the ice, and she heard a terrible ripping sound. It was the sound of her blade hitting a hard curve. She landed too late!

Her skate slipped from underneath her, and before Eva knew it, she was falling, headfirst onto the ice.

Then everything went black.

CHAPTER 3

REST

At the doctor's office, Eva felt a little seasick. Like she needed to throw up. The car ride must have been really bumpy.

"You have a concussion," the doctor said. "Nothing too bad, but you do need to take it seriously."

"I just bumped my head on the ice," Eva said. "I fall all the time."

The doctor sat back in her chair. "This is not like the other times. This fall caused a mild traumatic brain injury. It causes temporary changes in the way your brain will work. If you don't take care of yourself, you can cause further damage."

Eva felt a little dizzy, but she didn't think it was too bad. "Is this going to affect my skating?" she asked.

Eva's mom frowned. "Taking care of yourself is more important than getting back in the rink, Eva."

The doctor looked at her charts. "Keep a close eye on your daughter for the next couple of days. If Eva starts to have serious vomiting or trouble waking up, bring her back to the hospital right away. I think a seven- to ten-day break from skating will be enough recovery time."

Eva sat up. The movement almost made her fall over. "That's an entire week off the ice!" she cried.

The doctor shuffled her papers. "Now that you've had a concussion, you are more likely to get them. It is very important that you get proper rest. Physical and cognitive."

"Cognitive?" Eva said.

The doctor nodded. He explained, "This means also resting from doing too much thinking activity, like computer or cell phone use, reading, or schoolwork."

Eva brightened. "I don't have to do homework!" she said.

The doctor chuckled. "Yes, you can skip homework for a couple of days. And I suggest you stay home from school tomorrow. Don't worry, though. We'll get you back on the ice soon."

During the car ride home, the excitement of not having to go to school wore off. Even if it meant taking a break from homework, it also meant staying out of the ice-skating rink.

How was she supposed to not skate for an entire week? She had been ice skating almost every day for as long as she could remember.

She thought of the axel jump. How stiff her body felt in the air. She remembered the feeling of the hard ice when she hit. She remembered the pain in her head. She could feel it right now.

Mom glanced over. "Why don't you tell me what happened today at practice?" she said.

Eva shrugged. "I tried a jump and fell. People fall all the time."

"Coach Jo said you didn't warm up," Mom said. Even though Mom kept her eyes on the road, it still felt as if Mom were watching her.

Eva stared out the car window. She didn't know her coach could be such a tattletale.

"I don't know if warming up would have helped," Eva said finally. "I was so nervous, I probably would have fallen anyway."

Mom put a hand on Eva's shoulder. "You need to do your warm-ups so you don't get hurt. Cooldowns too."

Eva sank further into the seat. "Hey, Mom?"

"Yes?"

Eva looked at her mother. "Do you think we can

get something to eat? I left my backpack and lunch at the rink."

Mom gave her a small smile. "Of course we can. I'm sorry you got hurt. I'll stop lecturing you."

Mom snapped her fingers. "Tell you what. We're close to Chinatown. Why don't we pick up some pork buns to share with Ama? Maybe a dozen egg tarts too?"

Eva managed to smile back. Egg tarts were her favorite.

She was missing practice, school, and time with her best friend on the ice. But at least she got to have some of her favorite Chinese food and share it with her mom and grandmother.

* * *

When they got home, Mom had to make two trips back and forth from the car. The first trip was to help Eva into the house. She was still feeling a little dizzy. The second time was to get the food.

Standing in the hallway, Eva called out to her grandma. "Ama!" she said. "We're home! We have food! We have char siu bao!"

Eva knew Ama didn't understand most of her English words, but she could pick out char siu bao, the Chinese words for steamed pork buns. If Ama didn't know what Eva was saying, she might be able to smell the food when Mom brought it in. Eva loved the aroma of savory pork. Her stomach rumbled. She really needed to eat.

Ama was sitting at the kitchen table. She was folding origami. She had paper flowers of every size scattered all over the table.

"Nǐ hǎo," Eva said. Saying hello was one of the few Mandarin expressions Eva knew.

Ama looked up. "Nǐ hǎo," she said, her voice kind and lovely. Then she spoke some more. The words came out fast.

Eva didn't know how to pick out what she was saying. It hurt her head a little to try.

"I fell down today," Eva said. "I'm okay, but I need to rest. I can't do a lot of thinking."

She could tell that Ama didn't understand. Eva gestured with her hands and body. She twisted from her waist, to show herself taking off in a jump. Then she spread her arms out as if she were getting ready to jump. Eva thought that maybe she just looked like a flapping chicken.

"Then *bam*!" Eva hit the table with her hands. "I fell and smacked my head."

Ama looked confused. She spoke, making gestures of her own. Eva couldn't understand. Her head was really starting to ache. Maybe this was the overthinking her doctor warned her about.

Eva held her head. When was Mom coming back? Ama was not good for her concussion.

Ama looked worried. As she spoke, her words just came out faster and faster. They seemed to loop around Eva like spinning circles on the ice.

The front door finally opened, and Mom walked in with the food.

Ama spoke in rapid Chinese to Mom. She seemed to be upset.

Mom spoke to her, and finally Ama said, "Ah."

She sat down and patted the chair next to her. Eva realized her grandmother wanted her to sit down. She did.

Together they ate pork buns. Mom and Ama talked in Chinese while Eva sat quietly next to them. Normally she would have felt frustrated to be left out of the conversation. But with her head hurting so much, it actually felt nice to not think about what they were saying. Even if she knew they were talking about her.

Eva picked up an egg tart. She loved egg tarts. They were like mini custard pies. The crust was buttery and flaky. On top, the egg custard was smooth and shiny, like the surface on an ice-skating rink.

The custard was also bright yellow. This color reminded Eva of her dress for the family showcase. Thinking about the song she chose, she got excited to show her routine to Ama.

"I really hope I'm better soon," Eva said to her mother and grandma. "I really want to skate in the performance."

Mom and Ama stopped talking.

"You will be," Mom said.

Ama said something and picked up an egg tart. Eva looked to her mom for help.

Mom smiled. "Your grandmother said egg tarts are her favorite treats too."

Eva ran a finger across the sticky, sweet top. It reminded her of gliding on ice. She took a big, delicious bite.

Eva liked that she and Ama had the same taste in treats. She couldn't wait to share her dance number with her grandmother too.

CHAPTER 4

PATIENCE

Eva knew she wasn't supposed to get on the
ice, but that didn't mean she should skip out on her
figure-skating lessons.

"Are you sure you want to go back to practice
already?" Dad asked from behind the steering
wheel in the car. He yawned. It was early in the
morning, and he was driving her in his pajamas
and tennis shoes.

"It's only been five days," he added. "Maybe
resting would be best."

Eva climbed in the passenger side and shut the door. "I'm feeling better, and I already missed so much. Even if I can't get on the ice, at least I can do some moves outside the rink. Plus, we are both already out of bed and in the car!"

"That's true," Dad said, starting the car. He glanced at the clock on the dashboard. "Wow, I don't think we've ever left this early before. You must have hit your head harder than we thought, Eva."

"Ha-ha," Eva said. "You're such a comedian." Dad just grinned.

When they got to the ice-skating rink, Dad handed her a muffin. "Remember to not overwork yourself," he said. "Take it easy. We don't want you to reinjure yourself."

"I'll remember," she said. She opened the car door and got out. She only carried her book bag today. She'd left her skating bag at home.

But what Dad didn't know was that her figure

skates were hidden next to her schoolbooks in her bag. Eva *would* take it easy—easy on the ice.

When Eva reached the rink, there were already a few skaters warming up. She wished she could have been the first one on the ice.

Whenever she made it to the rink first, she got a thrill from being the only one skating. The rink felt so wide and big when no one else was on it, as if it were all hers. Eva loved the feeling of being out there on her own with no one watching.

She sat down on a bench and waved to Jazz. Out on the ice, Jazz was skating backward.

"Hi, Eva! It's so great to see you back at the rink where you belong," Jazz said. "Are you practicing today?"

Eva looked around to see whether Coach Jo was there before answering. The coast was clear.

She waved an ice skate in the air. "I'm going to try and get a few minutes in," she said. "I'll be there in a second."

Eva laced up her boots. She knew her parents would really be upset if they knew she was getting back on the ice. But she wasn't going to do any jumps. She would just do a couple of laps around the rink—just to get the feel of the ice. Perfectly safe and easy.

Eva walked onto the ice and caught up with her friend.

"Hey, watch this," Jazz said. "My lutz jump has really come along."

Jazz skated backward in a large circle, picking up speed in the rink. She paused and stood on her left leg, standing on the back outside edge of her skates. To maintain balance, her right side was angled back, right arm pointed toward the sky.

She glanced behind her. Bending her knee, Jazz jumped into the air, kicking her free leg back. She pulled her body into one counterclockwise rotation. Landing on her right leg, Jazz kicked her skate into the ice to hold her position. Holding her left leg out, she stood tall, nice and straight. She looked strong and beautiful.

"Way to go!" Eva cheered. "You nailed it."

Seeing Jazz jump made Eva feel fluttery inside. It had only been a few days away from the rink, but she had missed the ice so much.

This excitement made Eva skate faster. Before she knew it, she was gearing up to do a spin. Maybe one little twirl wouldn't hurt. She wouldn't be jumping, so there was really no risk of her falling.

Eva decided to do a twizzle, which is a spin that moves across the ice. She pushed forward with one foot and quickly spun, keeping her other leg held out. As she rotated across the ice, her arms were extended.

She hit her position just like she normally did. But this time, the quick spinning motion made the rink blur around her much faster than usual. It didn't feel the same. It didn't feel right.

Eva felt herself breathing faster. She felt like throwing up and quickly tried to stop herself from spinning. When she placed her other leg down, the rink seemed to tilt sideways. She was falling, and suddenly she felt the cold ice beneath her.

"Eva!" Coach Jo's voice came from above.

Eva looked up. She didn't realize Coach Jo was already on the ice, and now here she was standing over her, along with Jazz and a couple of other girls.

"Hi, Coach," Eva said, waving a gloved hand in the air.

Coach Jo helped her up. "You aren't supposed to be on the ice. I need to call your parents."

Eva groaned. This wasn't going to end well.

* * *

At home, Mom was in a rush. She was late for work and told Eva that she would not be going to school today. She would have to stay home with Ama. She wanted Eva to think about what she had done. There was to be absolutely no TV or screen time.

Eva spent most of the morning in her room, being careful not to listen to loud music or read anything. All she could do was sleep. She took a nap, and when she woke up, she decided to make a sandwich for lunch.

When she got into the kitchen, Eva saw Ama at the table. Around her were paper hearts, cranes, and flowers. Ama noticed Eva and motioned her over. Eva sat next to her grandmother.

Ama pushed a square of paper in Eva's direction. She folded it in half and waited.

"Oh, do you want me to follow you?" Eva asked.

Ama folded the paper in half again. The paper now had four squares.

"Okay, I guess you do," Eva said, taking her paper. She made the same folds her grandmother made.

Her first folds were slow and awkward. "You know, Ama," she said. "My fingers are a little clumsy for origami."

Ama simply waited for Eva to copy her motions. When Eva messed up, Ama waited. She folded her paper again, demonstrating what Eva should do.

After many folds, Ama and Eva both held kite shapes.

"Hey, we made little kites," Eva said with a small smile. "That's cool."

Ama shook her head. She continued on, unfolding the tops of the kite.

Eva watched, then did the same. Soon the kites transformed into something different. Something with a stem and petals.

Ama took a wooden chopstick and curled each of the petals around it. She handed Eva a chopstick, and Eva did the same. When she was finished, she had created a paper flower that looked just like a lily.

Ama said something in Mandarin. Eva didn't understand, but her grandmother sounded pleased. Eva nodded along.

Ama stopped and placed a hand on Eva's arm.

"Patience," Ama said. She smiled and gestured toward the paper flowers.

Eva looked at them. She looked at Ama.

"Patience," Eva said.

CHAPTER 5

THE RETURN

Eva looked at the clock. Taking one more day away from ice skating made her feel like she had missed an entire year. Even with the extra day of rest, she was still running late. This time, more than ten minutes. She slammed the car door shut and ran into the building.

"Not so fast, Eva!" Mom yelled from the car. "Don't overwork yourself!"

Eva slowed down slightly, then picked up her pace when she got out of Mom's sight.

Inside, Eva could see the other girls twirling and spinning. She spotted Jazz. Then Stephanie. Right then, Stephanie completed a perfect jump and landing.

Eva felt the room spin. Was she still feeling dizzy from her concussion? What was she doing there? Should she still be home in bed? She could barely walk without feeling sick. How was she ever going to get back on the ice?

Before she could answer the questions running through her mind, Coach Jo called out to her, "Hello, Eva!"

Coach Jo's voice was cheerful, as always. She was very tiny. Eva was almost taller than her. Despite her small size, Coach Jo always seemed bigger and taller on the ice.

"Hi, Coach," Eva said, jogging up to meet her. "I'm sorry I'm late. But now that I'm here, I'm not sure I should have come. I can't do anything on the ice anyway."

Coach Jo put one hand on her hip. "How are you feeling?"

"If I move too fast, I get a little dizzy," Eva said. She thought for a moment. Was she really not feeling well or was she anxious about not getting enough ice time? Finally she admitted, "It isn't so much that I'm not feeling well; it's more that I'm worried about not being ready for the showcase."

"Then it's good that you came in this morning," said Coach Jo. "There is still plenty you can do to prepare without getting on the ice, Eva. We're running through the entire show in order this morning. Even though you won't be able to skate, we can still play your song when it's your turn. That way you can still get the feel of your performance piece. You can practice the movements outside the rink."

With Coach Jo's help, Eva did some warm-ups and conditioning. Then Coach Jo told her she would move through her routine, just standing in one place.

"When your song comes on, I want you at the front of the rink," Coach Jo said. "Not on the ice, just on the ground. You can move your body to the music and still get in some practice."

Eva felt hopeful. While she couldn't put skates on her feet, she could still dance, in her own way. Eva listened to the first song and watched the other skaters.

Soon it was Jazz's turn. Eva gave a quick wave to her friend.

Jazz was getting ready for her salchow jump. She was turned backward, her black ponytail flying in the wind. Eva saw her step forward and turn on her skates three times. Jazz had great control. She held her left arm in front, with her right arm in back. She bent her knee as she prepared to jump. Springing off the toes of her skates, she rose into the air. She did one rotation and landed on her foot.

Jazz did her routine flawlessly. She was fast and powerful, like always.

Eva clapped. She watched other skaters do their numbers. She saw many jumps and wobbles. Finally it was time for her song.

Eva made her way to the floor area where the skaters typically waited to enter the ice rink. In her sneakers, she held her arms out and waited for the music.

The first notes came, and she started her routine. The melody was soft and beautiful. Then the lyrics started. Eva moved to the song. At first it felt strange to dance off the ice. She didn't feel as sick though. Moving on the floor, Eva realized she could still feel the rhythm of the song.

Eva did her spins and danced. She loved hearing the song around her. It was the first time she had heard it played in the rink. It felt like the words were just for her.

She was so caught up in the music that she was surprised to hear someone laughing. The sound broke her concentration. She looked around.

Eva saw Stephanie covering her mouth. *Are they laughing at my dancing?* Eva wondered.

Stephanie and two other girls had their heads together. They were smiling, but not in a friendly way. "What kind of a song is this?" Eva heard Stephanie say.

"It's not even in English!" another girl said.

Eva almost stopped dancing. The girls weren't poking fun at how she was dancing. They didn't care that she was doing her routine without her skates.

The girls were laughing at Eva because of her song. They were laughing because she was Chinese.

She remembered what she was doing and went through the motions of her axel jump, pretending to leap in the air. Even though she was moving, on the inside she felt frozen.

Continuing the dance number, Eva started to feel dizzy. She wasn't sure whether the sick feeling was from her head injury.

The song was coming to a close. Eva ended with the scratch spin, walking circles around on the floor in tight rotations as she would have on the ice. With her hands stretched in the air, Eva pretended not to hear their cruel remarks. But her heart hurt worse than her head.

It was an injury Eva wasn't sure how to fix.

CHAPTER 6

ALARMING

A few days later, Eva's alarm clock went off as usual. She groaned.

BEEP-BEEP-BEEP

Eva reached out and slapped the snooze button on her alarm clock. She glanced at the time:

4:45 a.m.

Today was her first practice back on the ice. The doctor had finally cleared her for skating. She closed her eyes.

Last night Eva had set the alarm to go off even earlier than her usual 5 a.m. wake-up time. She thought that if she got to the rink a little earlier, she could shake off any nervous feelings. Now that the day of practice was here, she wondered whether she wanted to get out of bed at all.

BEEP-BEEP-BEEP

5:05 a.m.

The alarm went off again. This time when she hit snooze, Mom came in the room. She switched on the overhead light.

"Mom!" Eva said, covering her eyes.

"Time to get up," Mom said, her voice too cheerful for five in the morning. "Coach Jo is expecting you bright and early today."

Eva threw off her blankets. She got her breakfast and school bag ready.

In the car, Eva's mom played her family showcase song. Hearing it didn't make Eva feel any better. She heard the Mandarin lyrics the way the other girls did. They sounded funny and strange. They reminded her that she had been laughed at. Not because she wasn't a good skater, but because she was ice skating to a Chinese song.

Eva's mom pulled up to the rink. "You got this, kiddo," she said.

Eva didn't unbuckle her seat belt. She could almost hear Stephanie's snickers. "I don't think I should go to practice today," she said. "I'm not sure if I'm fully recovered."

Mom held out her skates. "Where is my girl who snuck these into her book bag because she couldn't wait to get back on the ice?" she asked brightly. "The doctor said you're fine. Go on, Coach Jo is waiting for you. She is really happy with your progress."

After the car left, Eva looked back after her mother. For some reason, Snow Castle Ice Arena looked larger today. It felt colder. Eva wrapped her arms across her body. She was shivering.

Since she was on time, Eva walked slowly to the ice rink. Mom said Coach Jo thought she was doing great. Mom didn't know. She wasn't there to hear how people laughed at her Mandarin song. Instead of feeling proud of how far she had come since her head injury, Eva felt smaller.

She couldn't get the sound of the girls' laughter out of her head. She didn't see Coach Jo in the rink area. She didn't see Jazz practicing nearby.

All she could see was herself from yesterday. Frozen, near the ice while others laughed around her.

Eva stopped walking. Her bag felt heavy.

She heard laughing. It was Jazz's voice. She may have been talking with another skater, but Eva felt as if her best friend's laughter was aimed at her.

Part of Eva knew Jazz would never find humor in Eva's music or culture. Another part of her thought that everyone was laughing at the same joke.

One that made fun of her.

Instead of walking toward her friend, Eva took a step back. And then another.

Eva turned and slowly walked out of the rink area. She hid behind a row of seats. If she ducked between rows, she could stay out of sight but still watch practice. She stayed there. Huddled down and peeking out from the space between the chairs.

A whistle blew. It was time for the freestyle sessions to start. The skaters lined up. Some were finishing up their warm-ups. Others were ready to skate. Eva felt a longing to be on the ice with them.

She watched Coach Jo do a quick head count. Coach Jo looked around the rink. She might have been looking for Eva.

Eva tucked herself behind the chairs. She could see wads of gum stuck to the bottoms of the seats. She made sure not to touch them.

Eva didn't want Coach Jo to see her. How could she go back on the ice when everyone had laughed at her song? They weren't just making fun of the music. They were laughing at her for being Chinese.

She thought of Ama, the soft and beautiful way Mandarin sounded on her grandmother's lips. Eva realized the Chinese words didn't sound so graceful to other people.

This made Eva sad. What if people made fun of the song during the performance and Ama thought they were laughing at her? She didn't want Ama to feel the way she was feeling right now.

From her hiding spot, Eva could hear the familiar noise of blades on ice. The way the skates ground into the smooth surface was one of Eva's favorite sounds. She could almost feel herself doing it.

Eva had injured herself only a week ago. It felt a lot longer. She missed the way her boots fit snugly around her ankles. She missed the brisk wind on her face as she glided on the ice. She missed dancing to the music and jumping in the air.

She watched the skaters do their routines.

Eva marveled at how good they looked. Their form was strong. Their balance and posture confident. Even the ones who made mistakes still looked as though they belonged on the ice.

For the rest of the practice, Eva didn't come out from her hiding place. For the first time in her life, she didn't feel at home at the ice rink.

Eva felt stuck. She wanted to go home, but she also didn't want to leave. She could go out and practice her routine, but she was afraid of the laughter. She didn't know whether she could do her axel jump again. She didn't know whether she could even do her routine.

Eva wondered whether she would ever jump again.

CHAPTER 7

PEPPERMINT TEA

Eva came home from school and saw her mom seated at the kitchen table. In front of her were a teapot and two teacups.

"Hi," Mom said. She poured herself a cup of tea. "Come over here and sit down. How was school today?"

"Fine," Eva said, pulling out a chair at the table. She took off her backpack and sat it on the ground next to the chair. "I had a test in history, and I think I did pretty good."

Mom moved the other cup in front of Eva. The teacups were so pretty. White, with a pink cherry blossom print. They each rested on a small plate with the same pink flowers.

Eva slowly sat down and shrugged off her sweater. She realized the house seemed extra quiet. "Where's Ama?" she asked.

"She's at the community center," Mom said. She poured tea into Eva's cup. "They are offering an advanced origami class. They are making a Chinese dragon. Ama was pretty excited about it when I dropped her off."

Eva smiled. Ama had been very patient with Eva while teaching her how to make the simpler paper lilies. She knew the challenge of making a more complicated dragon would be fun for Ama.

Eva raised the cup of tea to her nose. She took a big sniff. It smelled minty and not very sweet. "What kind of tea is this?" she asked.

"Peppermint," Mom said. She took a sip of her own. "It's supposed to help with anxiety and help you feel calm. The mint should be soothing to your whole body. It may help clear out anything that is causing stress."

Eva took a small sip and made a sour face. The tea was very bitter. Minty, but not much taste after that.

Mom gave a small laugh and moved the bowl of sugar toward Eva. "Not sweet enough for you?" she asked.

"Not quite," said Eva. She spooned sugar into her teacup and gave it a big stir. "I didn't know you were anxious," she added. "What's got you so worried?"

"Oh, I certainly worry about things, but I'm probably not as nervous as you," Mom replied.

Eva looked up. "What do you mean?"

Mom set her teacup down. "Coach Jo said she didn't see you at practice this morning."

"Oh." Eva took a long drink. "So this tea is for me then."

"When I picked you up for school, you didn't mention that you hadn't gone to practice," said Mom.

Eva's face felt hot. "I did go to practice, but I just watched. I couldn't go out there."

"I don't understand," Mom said. "Just a few days ago, you were sneaking your skates in your bag to go to practice. But now that you are free to skate again, you hide from your coach?"

"I think I need more time to rest," Eva said. "Maybe I shouldn't go back to practice for a while."

Mom added honey to her tea and stirred slowly. "You seem to be really worried. Can you tell me about it, Eva?"

Eva couldn't find the words to say. She kept hearing Stephanie's snickers.

"What are you thinking about?" Mom asked.

Finally Eva spoke. "Everyone was laughing at

me, Mom." She heard her voice, and it sounded as small as she felt.

"Oh sweetie," Mom said. "It was unfortunate that some of the girls weren't understanding about your practice situation."

Eva looked up. "No, Mom. They weren't laughing at my accident. They were laughing at my song. They were making fun of me for being Chinese."

Saying the words made Eva feel dizzy again. She made swirls in the tea with her spoon. They went around and around, like a mini tornado. Eva felt as though she were swimming in it.

Mom set her cup firmly down on the table.

"I had no idea," she said. "That sounds terrible. I'm so sorry."

Eva couldn't look up from the whirlwind. She felt like a baby. She tried to think about something else, but her thoughts froze. Just like what had happened at practice.

Her mother took Eva's spoon and placed it in the center of her tea. The swirling stopped.

Mom held out a hand and tipped Eva's chin up. "Your Chinese song is beautiful. Just like you," she said.

Eva met her mother's eyes. They were dark brown, just like hers. "Do you really think so?" she asked.

Mom took out her phone. She scrolled through the music section and began to play a song. It was Eva's song.

Mom quietly hummed along to the Mandarin words. She was right. The song *was* beautiful.

It may not be powerful and upbeat like Jazz's song. Or classical and strong like Stephanie's. It was unique and lovely. Just like Eva.

She drank some of her tea. It was warm in her belly. It felt nice.

With the sugar, it was no longer bitter. It tasted just right.

"I'm sorry for skipping out on practice today," she said. "I'll try again."

Mom stopped the song. She finished her tea. Then she looked Eva straight in the eye. "You can do this, Eva," she said. "I know you can."

Eva finished her tea. "I know I can too."

CHAPTER 8

THE AXEL JUMP

Eva spent the next weekend doing fun things that were not related to figure skating.

One night Ama taught her how to make origami animals. They made a horse, a frog, and a bird. Even though they couldn't easily talk back and forth, it was fun to be in the room together. While they folded paper, Mom made them mint tea.

On Saturday Jazz came over. Dad took them to get doughnuts, and it was nice to have someone besides her family to hang out with.

While at home, Eva and Jazz painted their fingernails. They wanted to experiment with styles and decide how they would do them for the performance.

Jazz chose to go with multicolored nails with shiny sparkles on one hand. It suited her personality.

Eva went with a sunshine yellow nail polish. She knew it would match her outfit. She used silver glitter at the tips of her fingers.

When their nails dried, Eva made Jazz some tea in the kitchen. Holding her teacup up, Jazz stuck her pinkie finger out. It was painted in neon pink and had a sparkly racing stripe down the middle of it. Eva giggled when Jazz moved it back and forth.

"I'm so glad you are finally coming back to practice! Are you just so excited for Monday to finally get here?" Jazz said. She squeezed a lot of honey into her cup.

When she passed over the honey bear,
Eva shook her head. She decided to stick with
sugar. She took a tiny sip of tea. "I don't know,"
she said.

Jazz leaned back in her chair, her teacup in
her hands. "I didn't realize you hit your head that
hard," she said.

Eva looked down into her cup. Jazz was her best
friend. She needed to remember she could share her
most painful feelings with her. "It isn't just getting
hurt that is making me not want to skate," Eva
started.

Jazz blinked. "Oh?"

Eva took a deep breath. "During my routine,
I heard some girls laughing at my song. They were
making fun of it because it's in Chinese."

Saying these words out loud hurt, almost more
than her concussion headaches. At the same time,
it was also a relief, as if she had been holding her
breath and finally let it go.

Jazz narrowed her eyes. "Those jerks," she said. "What do they know? They all skate to the same boring songs. It's almost like they're scared to try something new."

Eva looked up. "So you don't think my song is stupid?"

"Not at all!" Jazz said. "I've heard everyone else's songs a million times. I'm falling asleep right now just thinking about listening to the same songs again."

Jazz closed her eyes and fake snored.

Eva giggled.

Jazz sat up. "Your song is new and different," she said. "I'm so glad it's in the program. You're bringing something new to the rink, and the fans will love it!"

Eva smiled. "Thank you," she said.

Jazz took a drink. "It's like this tea," she said.

Eva snorted. Mint tea almost went up her nose. "What are you talking about?" she asked.

"Your routine and music are like the tea. Minty, fresh, and new," Jazz explained. She held out her teacup. "Cheers to you, Eva. Thanks for bringing something unique to the rink. It gave me ideas."

Eva clinked her cup with Jazz's. "Oh, yeah?"

"Yeah! Maybe for my next number, I'll skate to an all-percussion piece." Jazz tapped out a rhythm on the tabletop. "Just the bad bass drops and the beats!"

Eva giggled. Jazz could always make her laugh. "If anyone could pull that off, Jazz, it's you!" she said.

Jazz fluttered a brightly colored hand in the air. "You are really brave to use a song that is so important to you. Don't forget that," she told Eva. "Even though you know some people might be dumb about it, you're sticking by your song. It would be easy to just change songs, but it wouldn't be right."

Eva thought for a minute. Jazz was right. While she was upset that the girls had laughed at her song, she had never thought to pick something else for her routine. True, she had considered not skating at all. But taking the Chinese song out of the program was never an option.

"I'm also really scared about doing the axel," Eva said. "I don't want to fall again."

"Well, if you're really scared, maybe you don't have to do it," Jazz said.

Eva hadn't thought about that before. Coach Jo really wanted her to showcase her skills. She wanted Eva to show the audience and herself what she was capable of this season. Eva was supposed to show Ama her hardest jump. But Eva didn't know whether she could do it.

She sloshed the tea around her cup. It had gotten cold.

"I guess I could skip the axel jump for now," she said.

"I'm sure you'll make the right decision," Jazz said. With one big gulp, Jazz finished her tea. "Time to paint our toes now."

Eva put her cup in the sink and pretended to be excited about getting ready for the performance. But she wondered whether she could do it at all.

CHAPTER 9

CHANGE OF ROUTINE

At practice the next morning, Eva told Coach Jo about her new plan.

"I'm not sure if doing the axel is the right move right now," Eva said. She picked at the stitches in her glove. She couldn't meet her coach's eyes. She was worried about letting the coach down.

Coach Jo studied Eva. "I understand," she said. "The axel is a frustrating jump, especially after an injury. You know, when I was your age, I think I felt the same way about scratch spins."

Eva looked up. "Really? They're so easy."

Coach Jo watched the other skaters on the ice. "Not for me," she said. "I didn't like how it felt to spin so fast. I still don't. Doing them reminds me of the time I was in a scratch spin and I couldn't seem to slow down. The tighter my spins got, the more out of control I felt. I fell and cut my lip pretty bad."

She pointed to a faint scar on her face that Eva had never noticed.

Coach Jo skated away from Eva and started to rotate. Her limbs came together into a beautiful scratch spin. She held her arms up. Her body twirled, from the tops of her fingers to the bottoms of her toes. She was a tornado of speed and spinning. She quickly stopped and faced Eva.

Eva clapped. "I don't know what you're talking about. You're great at scratch spins," she said.

"Even now, I still wonder if I'm going to remember how to stop," Coach Jo said. "I understand how hard it is to overcome a fear, Eva. The best way is to face it. Even if you fall."

She skated back toward Eva. "What do you say? How about you face the axel jump and just do your best?" she asked.

Eva thought of Ama. She wanted to show her the jump. She nodded once.

Eva pushed off with her skates, searching for her power. She turned her body in preparation for the axel. She felt the moment coming.

But then Eva hesitated. Instead of launching herself into the air, she never left the ice. She skated right through the jump.

Coach Jo was next to her. "You wanted to do it, Eva," she said. "I saw the setup."

Eva's face felt warm. "I know," she said. "It just makes me really nervous."

"Okay, so what about it makes you nervous? What are you afraid of?" Coach asked.

"Well, I could fall," said Eva.

"You know what to do when you fall," said Coach Jo.

"I know, I know," Eva said. "Lean into the fall, don't extend my hands."

"I mean you get back up." Coach smiled.

"Oh, right," said Eva.

Coach Jo nodded. She pointed to the right side of the rink, where the music sound system was. A teenage boy pointed at her and put on headphones.

"I got you some time with your song," Coach Jo said. "I'm going to go watch from outside the rink. I want you to do your number. You know your routine. Take it slow. Go for those jumps."

Eva nodded quickly. This is why she was at practice. She was here to get better.

Eva skated toward the middle of the rink. Even with the other students gliding around, she pretended she was alone on the ice.

The song started. Familiar chords in a song she had heard countless times. Eva spread her arms wide. Then the lyrics in Chinese came. The Mandarin words were strong and beautiful. Eva felt her body moving to the music.

As she practiced her routine, Eva felt the movement of other skaters around her.

"Ching chong song dong," a girl said, giggling as she skated by.

Eva froze. The mocking words took her out of the music. She heard Stephanie laugh.

"Keep going, Eva!" Coach Jo called from the side. She hadn't heard Stephanie and the other girls being mean.

"You got this, Eva!" Jazz shouted from the other end of the rink. She also hadn't heard anyone making fun of her Chinese song.

Eva narrowed her eyes. She *had* heard it all, but she wasn't going to let those cruel comments chase her away. She sped up, leaving the hurtful feelings behind. She leaned into her spins, her footwork, and her turns.

When it was time for her first jump, Eva tilted herself backward to set herself up. All she could hear was music. She leapt.

Spinning in the air, she was swept away by the thrill of the jump. Her right foot touched the ice and she landed. Then she fell.

"It's just a fall!" Coach Jo shouted from the sides. "You were still great!"

Eva felt the cold ice through her gloves. She didn't feel great. She got up and tried again. Eva spent the rest of the practice slipping and falling. She made some jumps, but missed more. By the end of practice, she was sore.

As Eva took off her skates, Coach Jo sat next to her. "The performance is this weekend. I think you're ready, but you have to feel that way too."

Eva tucked the laces into her boots. "I'm not sure if I am," she said.

"I'll let you decide," Coach Jo said. "Right before you get on the ice, I want you to make a decision. Commit to the jump or leave it out. Either way it will be a great routine."

Eva nodded. She knew the jump was possible, but she wasn't sure. Before she got on the ice, how would she know whether she could do it?

CHAPTER 10

THANK YOU

Eva peeked at the crowd. The seats were filled, and the arena was full of families. She spotted her mom and dad sitting in the front row. Where was Ama?

Eva paced around the outside of the rink. Coach Jo had said she could decide to do the axel jump or take it out. She still didn't know what to do. As she walked back and forth, Eva heard someone speaking in Chinese.

Then Jazz's voice.

"Uh, Eva?" Jazz said. "I think your grandma is looking for you."

Eva saw Ama smile, then wave.

Eva walked over to her. "What are you doing back here, Ama?" she asked.

Ama patted Eva's arm. She said words Eva didn't understand. Ama then reached into her bag and pulled out a large bouquet of flowers—origami flowers.

There were lilies, roses, and green leaves, all in a beautiful paper bundle. It looked so delicate and strong at the same time. This was the perfect present for Eva.

"Oh my goodness," Eva said as Ama handed her the flowers. "Xiè xiè, Ama. Thank you."

Ama smiled. "I love you," she said in perfect English.

Eva hugged her. "I love you too, Ama."

Coach Jo came up to them. "Eva, you're up soon."

She looked at the flowers. "What a beautiful bouquet!"

Eva couldn't help but grin. "Ama made them for me."

Coach Jo nodded. "They really are lovely."

She turned toward Ama and said something in Mandarin.

Ama smiled widely and spoke back. They exchanged words for another minute.

"Oh my gosh, Coach Jo!" Eva said. "You can speak Chinese!"

Coach Jo laughed. "I thought you knew that. It's one of the reasons why I am so happy to see you skate to the Coldplay song today. I love 'Yellow,' and those Mandarin lyrics too."

Coach Jo took Ama by her arm. "Eva, you have a few more minutes before you go on the ice. I'm going to help your grandmother find her seat. You get ready."

"Got it, Coach."

Even though she had warmed up before, Eva did some stretches. She was going to be fully prepared this time. As she pulled her arms behind her head, Stephanie and another girl came walking up to her.

They were looking down at their hands.

"Hi, Eva," Stephanie said.

"Hello." Eva kept her voice cool.

Stephanie could barely meet Eva's eyes. When she finally looked up, Eva saw that she looked sad. "I wanted to say how sorry I am about laughing at your song. My coach explained to me how rude I was during practice this week. I know it wasn't right."

"Me too," the other girl said. "It was wrong of me to make fun of the words like that."

Eva looked at the girls. They had hurt her. She would never forget how their laughter stung. But she also knew that this memory did not have the power to continue to hurt her if she didn't let it.

"I appreciate your apology," she said. Her voice was a little warmer. "Good luck on your performance."

"You too," Stephanie said. She looked relieved. "By the way, I really like your nails."

Eva looked at her glittery yellow nails. Jazz would be happy to know her work was noticed. "Thank you," she said.

The family showcase was about to start. The younger skaters went first. It was fun to see figure skaters of many ages on the ice. Eva remembered when she first started. She thought about how far she had come. She could even do the axel jump now.

Remembering this made Eva feel confident. She really had learned a lot. She was glad she decided to stick with figure skating. Even with the early morning practices, and even with the hard times. Even with the falls.

Right then she knew what she had to do.

When Jazz finished her number, Eva clapped and cheered loudly. When Stephanie skated, she also applauded. One by one, all the girls who were in front of her did their performances. Finally it was Eva's turn.

She made her way to the center of the rink.

Being alone on the ice gave her a special feeling. White ice, the color of bao buns, stretched all around her. It felt cool and familiar, and Eva knew this was where she belonged.

She thought about the song she had chosen, and that in just seconds Ama would hear it. She was going to dance to a song that Ama would understand. Thinking about her grandmother made Eva feel warm inside. Even warmer than drinking a cup of mint tea.

The music started. "Yellow" came through the speakers, and Eva started to dance. She could feel everyone watching her. She knew that somewhere out there, Ama was watching, and listening too.

When the lyrics began, the Mandarin words were sweet and beautiful. Eva held her arms out wide, as if to welcome the crowd into her song and dance. She wanted people to hear the soft sounds of the Chinese language. She hoped they were being moved by the music just as she was.

Eva glided across the ice with her spins and turns. She was in perfect time with the music. The routine was coming so naturally. As if she knew it by heart.

She knew an important part of her dance was coming up. It was time for her first jump. Eva turned to prepare for the axel.

She paused for a moment, then turned to glide backward. She stepped forward with her left leg to take off. As she pushed into the jump, Eva's arms and right foot went back.

Jumping straight up, she took off with her toe pick, her right knee rising. Her arms met in front. She pushed her right leg back and turned, launching her body off the ice.

Crossing her left leg, Eva brought her arms close to her body. She spun one and a half times, so fast she could hardly breathe.

To keep her balance when she landed, Eva made sure to keep her body weight on her right side. Her right toe came down, the toe pick grabbing the ice. She made the axel jump!

Eva balanced on her right foot, her arms held out in victory.

She heard the cheers and clapping from the crowd. Eva had landed her hardest jump. The song continued, and Eva floated through the rest of her routine.

She moved gracefully and powerfully. Strong and confident. Unique and lovely, just like herself.

Eva finished the song with a scratch spin, twirling her body close. She raised her arms as far as she could. When she finished the dance, she crossed her legs and bowed.

She could see her parents and Ama in the front row. They were standing and yelling for Eva. Ama held the origami bouquet in her hands. She waved it in the air, paper flowers blowing in the wind.

Eva raised a hand and blew a kiss.

"Xiè xiè, Ama," she said. "Thank you."

Veeda Bybee grew up collecting passport stamps and dreaming of castles in far off places. A former journalist, she has an MFA in creative writing from the Vermont College of Fine Arts. She lives with her family in Nevada, where she reads, writes, and bakes.

GLOSSARY

classical (KLAS-ih-kuhl)—relating to serious music in the European tradition

cognitive (KOG-ni-tive)—relating to mental activities, such as thinking, reasoning, remembering, and using language

concussion (kuhn-KUHSH-uhn)—injury to the brain due to jarring from a hit or fall

Mandarin (MAN-duh-rin)—standard Chinese language

motivation (moh-tuh-VAY-shuhn)—reason to act or accomplish something

parallel (pair-uh-LEL)—lying or moving in the same direction and always the same distance apart

personality (pur-suh-NAL-i-tee)—combination of emotions and behavior that makes a person unique

rotation (roh-TAY-shuhn)—complete turn around a center or axis

revolution (rev-uh-LOO-shuhn)—single complete turn around a center or axis

tempo (TEM-poh)—speed at which a musical piece or passage is to be played or sung

traumatic (truh-MAT-ik)—referring to a major bodily injury

DISCUSSION QUESTIONS

1. What do you think is the main conflict in the story? What other conflicts take place in the story?

2. Stephanie and the other girls made fun of Eva's culture. How would you explain to Stephanie why her actions were wrong and hurtful?

3. Have you ever suffered an injury that required recovery time? How did your experience compare with Eva's experience?

WRITING PROMPTS

1. Briefly research concussions. What dangers did Eva risk by getting back on the ice too early?

2. Think about successful athletes. What are some of the traits all successful athletes share? Write an essay about two or three of these traits, using examples from the story to support your points.

3. Imagine you are Eva and write a thank-you note to your grandmother for her support, using specific examples from the text.

LEARN THE TERMS

axel jump: Considered the most difficult of the jumps to master because of its forward takeoff. For a single axel, skaters use a forward outside edge takeoff, rotate one and a half times in the air, and land on the back outside edge of the other foot. The jump is named after Axel Paulsen, who first performed this jump in 1882.

camel spin: In this spin, the skater is bent forward with a free leg parallel to the ice, extended backward.

crossovers: These are performed by crossing one foot over the other while skating. The move helps skaters gain momentum or turn corners.

edges: Angles made when the blades touch the ice. Performed forward and backward.

gliding: Pushing off with one skate and gliding on the other.

mohawk: A turn in figure skating that involves a change of feet, but not a change of edge. It can be done on either inside or outside edges, forward or backward.

moves in the field: Skill test that includes more difficult edge and step patterns. Also, the elements of figure skating to show basic skills and edge control.

salchow: A jump in which the skater starts on the back inside edge of one skate and lands on the back outside edge of the other skate. A single salchow is one full rotation. This jump is named after Ulrich Salchow, who invented the move in 1909.

stroke: A method of moving across the ice in which a skater pushes off, using the inside edge of the blade, and alternates feet.

toe pick: The jagged edge at the toe of the blade.

waltz jump: A half-rotation jump made by taking off from a forward outside edge. This is the first jump that skaters learn.

FOR MORE ACTION
ON THE ICE,
PICK UP . . .

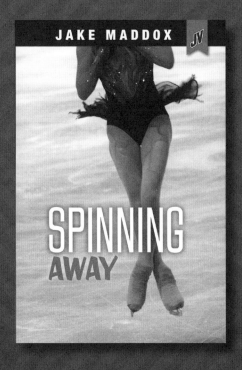

JAKE MADDOX · JV

SPINNING
AWAY